I'm NOT SCARED

An Imprint of Sterling Publishing
387 Park Avenue South
New York, NY 10016

Author: Dan Crisp
Illustrator: Lee Wildish

ISBN 978-1-4351-4898-7

Manufactured in Shenzhen, China
Lot #:
2 4 6 8 10 9 7 5 3 1
06/13

I'm NOT SCARED

Dan Crisp   Lee Wildish

Sandy Creek
NEW YORK

I'm not scared of MONSTERS. They don't frighten me.

Even ones with **scary eyes**;

I'd let them dine with me!

I'm not scared of GIANTS,

hanging out in the wild.

Even if they're man-eating beasts, and I am just a child.

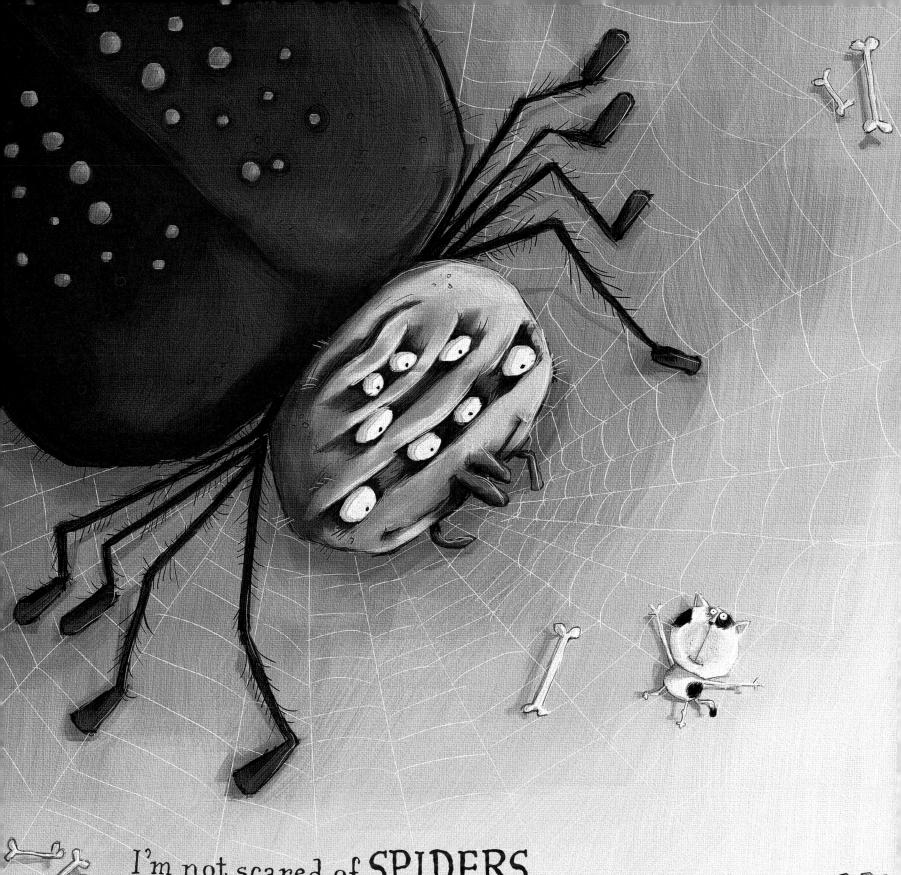

I'm not scared of SPIDERS,
be they as **big as a bus.**

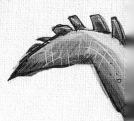

Cornered by a crowd of

CROCS;

I wouldn't make a fuss.

I'm even fine with WITCHES, as evil as they can be.

GHOSTS, GHOULS, and VAMPIRES –

they don't frighten me!

I'm not scared of SKELETONS,

rattling all their old bones.

Or strange sounds from the cellar;
the creepy moans and groans.

I'm not scared of **OGRES** and their great big **beady eyes.**

Lurking under bridges; they can't make me cry.

The
lions

and the
tigers,

great grizzly bears too.

They don't scare me **one little bit...**

how about you?

I'm not scared of JELLYFISH,

SHARKS, or

WRIGGLING EELS.

I turn my back and swim away,

kicking with my heels.

I'm not afraid of DRAGONS,

with their fire and scaly skin.

ROARING, *SCREAMING*, and jumping around –
all I do is grin.

I might be scared of **DINOSAURS**,
if they were still around.

Hang on there just a minute.

What's that
funny sound?

You'll have to please excuse me;
there's someone at the door . . .

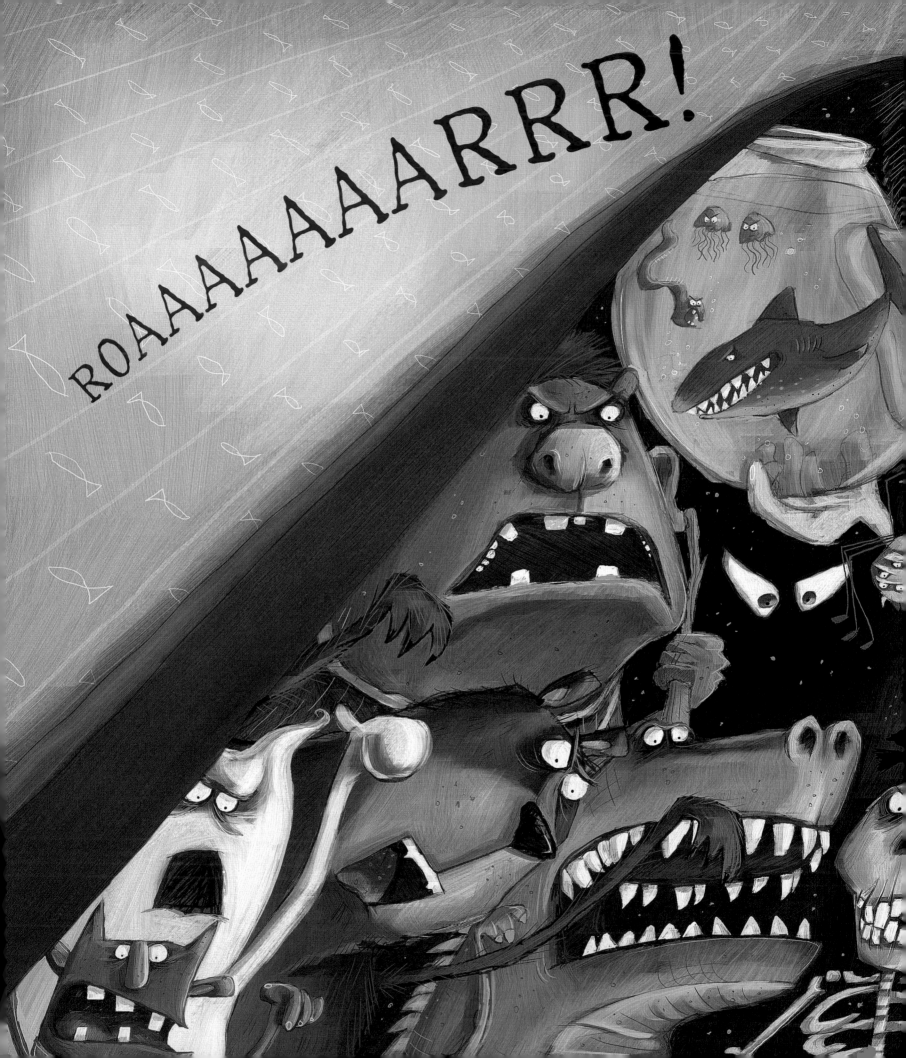